# Dawning Dusks

# Flairs and Glairs
Publication House

*"Dawning Dusks"*

# ISBN No: " 978-93-91302-70-2"
## 1st Edition
Language – English and Hindi

# Flairs and Glairs
## Publication House
## Regd. Under MSME Act.

# Disclaimer

This is a work of fiction and solely represent the thoughts of the corresponding authors of the articles. Our editors have tried their best to edit the content of all the authors and check the plagiarism.

All the write-ups in this book are unique and are only published in this book.

In case any plagiarism or error is found, only the author is responsible alone, and not the publisher or the Compilers.

**Cover Designing and Book Formatting**
*Shubham Shah and Ishani Agarwal*

# Co - Authors

**Shubham Shah (Founder Flairs and Glairs)**
**Ishani Agarwal (Co-Founder Flairs and Glairs)**
**Rutba Binti Hilal (Compiler)**

1. Aina Zulfikar
2. Arya. S. Nair
3. Amir Bashir Jan Sheikh
4. Afifa Jardosh
5. Azra Jan
6. Aqsa Andrabi
7. Asmat Bashir
8. Atif Shah
9. Bisma Rasheed
10. Giulia Sarro
11. Garima Pandey
12. Himanshi Yadav
13. Heena Farooq
14. Hafsa Khursheed
15. Ilsa Shafi
16. Ishrat Ashraf
17. Jasmine Panda
18. Krishnaveni
19. Maheena Zehra
20. Mohsin Bhat
21. Mir Mohammad Adnan
22. Misbah Mehraj
23. Mohammad Akram
24. Maleeha Sofi
25. Misbah Dar
26. Qurat Ul Ain
27. Ranivah Khursheed

28. Roonaq Fayaz
29. Sundus
30. Sayiba Hilal
31. Shafaq Qadri
32. Sahil Shakeel
33. Smriti Suman
34. Taha Gazala
35. Toufeel Chalkoo
36. Toiba Bilal
37. Yogesh
38. Zaid Jardosh
39. Zara Ayman Soofiyan

# Shubham Shah

## (Founder- Flairs and Glairs)

Shubham Shah, an entrepreneur at "Flairs & Glairs" a brand with dynamics in events organizing and cultural educational pan INDIA, is a 26yrs old guy who recently has entered the digital platform of imprinting emotions. He has initiated with his own open mic platform to help budding poets and aspiring writers under his brand named as "Teekhe Zasbaaat"

He is a commerce graduate from the Bhagalpur City of Bihar. He states Writing has impersonated him since childhood and he has now been writing for over a decade!
Cooking, on the other hand, is his passion! He also mentions, trying out new things just tickles him!
When asked sir, Why SPICY EMOTIONS?
He smiled and added, "agar jasbaat teekhe na ho toh wo jasbaat kahan" Spices are all that blends! So do his words!
As a chef, he presents to you his dish! Hot and freshly served! Taste it! Feel it! Enjoy it! You can also find his writing in the Book "Teekhe Zasbaaat" and 50+ Co-authored anthologies. With his passion to explore opportunities across Platforms, he is working with keen devotion and We wish him all the very best for his future ventures.
He is Featured in the International Magazine DeMode for his upcoming solo novel.
He is Approved by Ne8x for its Lit Fest, and is a Golden Star Awards 2020 Winner.
He is a India Book of Records Holder for his Anthology Satrang, and has the Grandmaster title by Asia Book of Records, for the same.
He has also been featured in Prabhat Khabar, Dainik Jagran, and a lot of other Newspapers in Bihar for his achievements.
He has been a proud co-author to
India Book Of Records (Title- Black)
World Book Of Records (Title -15 Wonders of Poetries)
India Book Of Records (Title - Aaina)
Vajra World Records Holder (Title - Gustakhi Maaf Hai)
High Range of Records Holder (Title - Gustakhi Maaf Hai)
Indian Book of Records
(Title - Road from Worst to Best)

Share your reviews on his

INSTAGRAM

@spicy_emotions
@shubham4shah

Or via email on

shubham2shah@gmail.com

To stay tuned to his work and opportunities follow his business Handles

INSTAGRAM          FACEBOOK           YOUTUBE

@flairsandglairs
@teekhezasbaaat

WEBSITE:

https://flairsandglairs.in/
https://flairsandglairs.com/

# Ishani Agarwal

## (Co-Founder- Flairs and Glairs)

Ishani Agarwal hails from the City of Joy, Kolkata.

She is the co-founder of her Community "Teekhe Zasbaaat" and Flairs and Glairs Publication.

Been a Compiler for 45+ Anthologies, she is in the process for more. Co-authored in 150+ Anthologies. She is a India Book of Records Holder, a Vajra World Records Holder, a High Range of Records Holder, an OMG Book of Records Holder, a Bravo Record holder, a Forever Star Book of World Records and an Indian Book of Records Holder.

Approved by Ne8x for its Lit Fest 2020, and Literary Icon 2020. Also a Golden Star Awards Winner 2020.

She has also been awarded with India Star Republic Award 2021, a part of She Awards by Awards Arc and Winner of Nari Samman 2021 by Literoma.

She is also selected as Best Achiever of the Year by AwardsArc and Most Challenging Compiler Award by Spectrum Awards.
She got her first solo Published,a solo Compilation consisting of first 750 contents of hers, titled "Hand That Burnt While Healing".

She has been featured by the National Magazine "Taree Zameen Par" with the title 'unstoppable'.
Also featured in the International Magazine DeMode for her upcoming solo novel, she is proud to write on social issues, and is happy with the love she is receiving.
Connect with her on Instagram: @Ishani_agarwal_quotes / @compilations_so_far

# RUTBA BINTI HILAL
# (COMPILER)

Rutba Binti Hilal
Daughter of Hilal Ahmad Sheikh and Sakeena Hilal.
She's a blogger, A Columnist and a writer Hailing from Drangbal region of Baramulla, Kashmir. Currently a class 11th medical student from Saint Joseph's Higher Secondary Baramulla, Kashmir.
She's a Weaver, Basically a word Weaver;
Who weaves her words so beautifully to make something eye soothing, Something to which heartbroken people relate, Her words are so enthusiastically filled with the chaos of every grief stricken person.
Well the world bleeds blood, But she bleeds ink.'

And She started bleeding the ink on paper when she was in class 9th. Furthermore She has also been the co-author of +15 books,
And after working in many anthologies she opted for publishing her own Anthology book 'DAWNING DUSKS'.
And despite Dawning Dusks, She's the compiler of another three books 'THE ALLURING BOND' 'RAVAGED SOULS' and 'MAYBE ONE DAY'.
And she's also working on her Solo debut book 'WEEPING IN THE VISIONS'.
And she believes that Writing is the lone path through which she converses with herself When nobody is there for tuning in. Her perspective related to writing is that paper has got more patience than people.

Mail ID: rutbabintihilal@gmail.com
IG Handle: @ruttbaaaa

# <u>She's Being Her Own Self</u>

To the spirits she is the strength,
To all the heights she is the length.
A woman carries the power to do the impossible,
A lady walks with the confidence for the unhappening things
to enable.

A touch of kindness,
A sprinkle of joyousness.
She walks with determination,
Her eyes shine with the interest of her ambition.

An angelic soul she seems to be,
Who allows her thoughts to flow free.
A motivator in her is always alive,
Who teaches not to give up and to always strive.

She won't follow the dark society with darker rules,
Because the society with unexceptional norms is the one who
always fools.
Yet; a strong being she stands out,
A soft voice with thoughts out loud.

She may be a sufferer from within,
But even the lost race she knows how to win.
Independent she is with her deeds high,
With the wings of courage she knows how to fly.
She has faith on her own self
She can solve her problems without seeking false help.
Always; to the spirits she is the strength,
To all the heights she is the length!

# Because She's A Girl

She is a girl,
She is being blazed, She is being burnt
Still she smiles, When it actually hurts.

She is a girl,
They call her whore, They call her slut
She stitched her mouth, And kept herself shut.

She is a girl,
She is being gazed, She is being raped
And they'll say, She can help the world to get shaped.

She is a girl,
She is being assaulted, She is being abused
And then they'll blame, She's accused

# <u>Dear Brave Me, I'm Proud Of You</u>

You went from; Zillion of throes,
Still you carry that smile;
Like a loaded gun, ready to explode.
And showed everyone;
That you are not going to feel glum,
And yes!
You became your own sun.
They made you feel like trash;
You developed proclivity for yourself,
They bullied you;
You turned the blinds eye,
They dragged you down;
You rose yourself
Yes! I do roger that,
You're going through the galaxies of torment and hoe
But sweetheart, It is in your fate;
What Else can you do?
You can't escape or make yourself go.
Precious,
You are a born girl and you have to feel low;
Because this is the damn world
And they think this way though.

# **<u>Power Up Women</u>**

There should be a hall fame,
Which women could claim.
All we need is to empower them;
Not focus on the length of her hem.

She might struggle, she might fall,
But isn't that life after all?
Why is she looked at as a doll?
And shown off at a dance hall?

I wish she was Hailed with grace.
And get her deserving place.
Only keep in mind, never to disgrace
Her name and claim in a public place.

After all she is a mother to someone,
A wife and a sister to another one.
And oh she means the world to one,
Not to forget the best friend to one.

She is the best creation of God.
And she also taught you to trod.
Oh how she saves you from fraud,
Only seen by her and you and God.

Power, respect, honour and praise,
Is due to her not only for days.
But for eternity, she'd be raise,
As a model of our prime days

# Aina Zulfikar

Hi Readers!
Her name is Aina Zulfikar and she  is 20 years of Age.
She is a writer, poet and is very passionate about writing and she is a social worker. She is also an Event Manager and working on Mental Health issues. She is currently pursuing b.com honors. And Aiming to reach out to all the people who are struggling in defeating anxiety, depression, and addiction to drugs.
Instagram handle @aina_zulfikar
@ainazulfikaraliii

# <u>Shredded Wings!  Rape Victim</u>

You took away from her, her childhood
You took away all that was good
You do it for your satisfaction
Do you even know how does it affect her
Her pain never lessens, not even a little but
Just keeps deepening, like a bottleless pit
Scary nights and painfull days
You destroy her in many ways
Thinking of hot panic that hijacked her soul
Destroying her was your only goal
Suffering and suffering with pain, guilt and hurt.
The pain she suffers because of your dirt.
The day has left a stain on her life
It kills her more than a knife.

# <u>Destroyed</u>

You raped her.
You trapped her.
Her soul is burning.
For peace she's yearning
She's unable to face the mirror.
You've filled her with terror.
She is completely isolated.
She is completely desolate.
She is alive, yet is so dead.
Her life is filled with a loose thread.
She is unmarried, yet a mother.
She prays the pain would catch no other.
You raped her, left her to die.
It's inexorably such a sigh.
She thinks about her broken dreams.
She is surrounded by her own screams.
You took away her happiness.
You destroyed her cheerfulness.
You forced her, you forced her.
You used her and you left her.
You killed her dreams, you killed her dreams.
You killed her dreams and filled her with screams.
Look her in the eye, you ravager.
Your existence should be filled with a frightening danger.
She's just nineteen and now she's bearing a baby.
All of this evil has made her crabby.
She is alive, yet is so dead.
Her life is filled with a loose thread.
She'll rise and be happy again.
She'll rise and be happy again.

# Arya. S. Nair

Arya. S. Nair is an MA English Student and a passionate writer. She has a blog page named GirlTalk where she publishes her writings. She is interested in dealing with various social issues, especially those concerning women and believes that writing is the best way to give voice to the suppressed. A keen advocate of equality, for her the world will become a better place only when people are respected regardless of their gender, caste or colour.

# <u>An Apology</u>

I screamed into your unhearing ears,
I kicked at your unfeeling flesh,
I shed tears before your blind eyes,
I begged you to let me go.

I begged you to look at me-
How my 12 year old body was twitching in pain
But all you did was beam with a heartless smile,
looking at my soiled bloody dress.

What did I do?
I never smoked with you,
I never drank,
I did not invite you with my smile.

I'm sorry I wore a skirt and played in the park,
I'm sorry I stepped out of my house,
I'm sorry I held your hand with faith.

I'm sorry.
I'm just a little girl
 who forced
an  angel like you
To become a devil
 by
just being me.

# Amir Bashir Jan Sheikh

Amir Bashir Jan Sheikh
The actual name of JS AMIR is Amir Bashir Jan Sheikh. 20 year old writer belongs to North Kashmir's Baramulla district. He is co author of two books "Dawning Dusks" & "Drowned Ink" He has got 1st & 2nd position in 10 & 12th respectively in the institutions he studied at . He also received Best Student Award in 12th class at Model HSS Boniyar.He is the student of Honours Political Science at DAV COLLEGE AMRITSAR.
Besides this he writes articles and runs his own YouTube Channel namely JS AMIR
Social Media Handles : JS_AMIR_
Email. amirbashirjansheikh121@gmail.com

# <u>Had No Mercy</u>

I curse I was wrong
With all sinful deeds that happened
In my sinless childhood
I felt guilt and stayed noiseless

I spoke and cry out for help
None of you approached for same
And mend your own business
I was left in the gloom

No one had clemency on me
He put me in the mental illness
And mutters of masses did same
Everyone insulted but no one assisted

Was I not a personage?
Didn't I belong to this planet
Yes! yes, we all are alike
But, why such lewdness with me

Day by day I grew older
I didn't listen to their abuses
I made myself plucky a lot
Forgot all and became queen of my world.

# **Brutal Return**

I fear, he may return
With all egotism and lust since morn
Will ambush the victims more
And impair their entity on a shore
He won't make a change. Oh! Such a rude
Lubricious and his senseless mood
Will ruin their gladness again
Put them in misery and pain
I shut my eyes and lockup my face
All time abashed with a disgrace
But not me, he was to blame for all
I spoke all time, no one attended my call
I approached all with same pain
Mostly I met who were insane
Sobbed a lot with curb less tears
He may advance everyone fears
Let's all make our voice one
Be hostile to such evil, wake and run
Today me, hereafter will be thou
Join hands and against this we all move.

# Afifa Jardosh

She is a wandering soul who finds herself in scribbling poetries, journaling and doing art with iridescent hues.

She drew her scars
She wrap her wounds
She wrote her flaws
She told her story
She wasn't fragile
Her skin screamed
The pain they gave
Her virginity they took
Without her assent
She wasn't afraid of
Her dreadful day which
Made her more stronger
They all can't take
What's within
She was, she is
More than a princess
A warrior, a knight of pen
A voice of unheard
She told her story
She didn't hesitate
She took her stand
She uttered to let 'em know
She is made of fire
She won't give up
Till she get justice
Till she sleep without nightmares
Till she read the statistics of such abuses is fallen down
Till she make all the women a power a revolution towards
the thinking of the society
Till she get heal as they didn't used her body but
They broke her soul
They fired her kindness
They killed her before death
They scratched her thoughts
They defeated her heart

But who knows
She is a wild stream
Not today but tomorrow
She will make her way home
She will make her way to sea
Where she belongs
And she will conquer the world
By her unabashed speech
To talk about women harassment
And to write thousands of articles on
making the pain as a power
She won
She become unstoppable
They didn't bothered her arms
They got the life of shame
They proved themselves they weren't manly man
She didn't hid
She let her story be
told and retold
Read and reread
For as we women's
Ain't made of crystals
And we don't know
What's called giving up

# Azra Jan

Azra jan is a poet hailing from the ganderbal district, she is currently preparing for medical entrance exams and does poetry in her part time.she believes one can express his/her hidden paint through words . She believes that poetry is a medium  by which one can easily express his/her feelings. For her poetry is like playing with the words of the soul.

The last rites of raped girl
The scars on the body created the memory
N the scars remind me ,  I am the abandoned soul
 I lost what i really was
N now it's the only regret of being a girl i have
My innocence was replaced by the worst pain
For the whole life i would have to own a dirty stain
In that dark room where he murdered my innocence n took
away my pride
That was the time where i really died
I stand with  u at every moment
But my soul is not now alive
As in the cage of vulgar man i was bound
The body of mine was in his hands to fill his lust
Where I owned the pain n he was in pleasure
I was yearning n he was vulgarly laughing
Breaking my breath slowly
While he was curious to capture my body
My tears and his sweat
My soul was broken while he proved as men
 i screamed ,yelled and cried hardly,with no sound
But He danced with my dead soul.

# Aqsa Andrabi

Syed Aksa Andrabi  was born on 28 March 1999 and hails from Pulwama. She completed her bachelor's in Actuarial and Financial Mathematics in January 2021. She is the author of the book "Mee_half : The Dispersed  Soul ".

Instagram ID @andrabi_aksa

(1)

A sardonic tale I carry within
Is yet to be opened
That is  agonized wholly
Like a deep pit of hell
Where I feel scars all over
Left by a brutal starter of my tale
The one who punched my body brutally
As cleavers laid on my body
Tearing my parts apart
And leaving a whole numbness in me
Where I could just scream all over
I feel as a dead corpse
Who can just have a bit of air
Waiting for a grave
To be laid in
with all my bruises.

(2)

A Blooming bud
Teared by some barbarous one
Just for the sake of his lust
Caged her soul within
With a sheer terror
Leaving her breathless
And a bud full of bruises
In a chaos she peers down her own
Drenched in a blood pool
Searching her torn parts all around
Bemoans all over
That never lessens
Couldn't abandon the frenzy world
He left her in.

# **Asmat Bashir**

Hey! Let me first give a brief description about myself. I'm ASMAT Bashir . I'm from sultanpora kandi, I'm a 15 year old girl. presently I'm in class 10th,studying at Guru nanak dev model high school baramulla.  I currently live in Kanispora Baramulla . Bashir Ahmad chopan is my dear  father And TASLEEMA Begum is my mother . Though I'm a full time student motivated by my parents and friends for learning and succeeding as I strive to become an outstanding and successful woman in today's society with the definative goal of becoming writer .I encourage fighting for what i desire  and believe in and doing it through God nothing is impossible if God is with you. I  haven't accomplished anything yet but I hope I'll achieve more success in my life.  Apart from above I have  a keen interest in cosmetology and I enjoy reading and writing short stories and poetry as well ,and most importantly spending my time with my loved ones . well!Now you might get to  know about my personality but I'm gonna  tell you something more about me. I like to have fun with my friends ,  sometimes I like to crack jokes with my friends. I am brave. friendly . I am quite interested in sports. I like badminton, long jump. and cricket .I'm also a funny person but only when I am in a good mood.let me tell you about my flaws. I'm a little bit of a forgetful person. I'm disorganized. I am a short tempered person . but ya I believe in spreading and giving love to people.!!!

# <u>She Is Strong Enough</u>

she is strong enough
to face her own journey!
just like moon and sun
her hopes springing high
she don't need any one to depend on
because she is reliable to everyone
she has spent endless night crying
she has been disappointed
but she is still strong
she can reach for the stars
let she repeat herself
she is more than what you see
because she is powerful beyond belief.

# Atif Shah

A silent, less participating and relatable writer.
Getting peace out of the words is the motive.

# <u>Just Because I Was A Girl</u>

I was the pride of the race,
But still I had to face
The hardships and crises ever,
For the rights whatsoever.
I was the thrown away pearl,
Just because I was a girl...
I fought and fought and fought,
For every right I never got.
First I fought for my birthright
In my mom's Womb with full might,
They thought my being a disgraceful hurdle,
Just because I was a girl...
I wanted to fly but they cut my wings
And handed me my wedding rings.
They made my wedding plans so great,
But at that stage I was only eight.
And my life was tied to this circle,
Just because I was a girl...
I fought for my right to education.
I just wanted to develop my nation.
But, does this nation even want me,
Then why this torture they can't even see.
For their dark minds, I was a burden
Just because I was a girl...
For such million reasons I fought,
But there was one I could never seek.
Many times humanity was trapped.
Many times I was raped.
Perhaps they think I can't quarrel,
Just because I was a girl...
The harassment I faced everywhere,
The body shames and whistles over,

The stage through which I'd to go,
None will ever do to his biggest foe.
Coz then I was a zoo-caged squirrel,
Just Because I was a girl...
But now things will change.
No more oppression ,no more cage.
I'll be free to fly,
Up to the heights of the sky.
I'll change my whole world,
Just because I am a girl…

# Bisma Rasheed

My name is bisma Rasheed and I hails from kanli bagh Baramulla.I recently completed Masters Degree in history.I am a writer and motivational quotes writer too.Actually writing was not part and parcel of my hobbies but my Inner emotions outer perception and creativity insisted me to pen down so.For me writing is just to play with an unheard voice, unheard feelings.Writing is just to express myself in my own way.

# **Speak Up Girl**

Speak up Girl
What are you Daunted of?
You are born free
You were born with a blaze inside you,
Your intramural emotions and sentiments are indispensable,
Don't Quash them Inside
When you speak ,speak with candidly , frankly and
fearlessly,
Speak up Girl
When you feel suppression and oppression,Don't
compromise.
Speak truth in your words and remain at your best,
Raise your voice
Your voice has an eminent power,
Don't be timid to use your power when needed
Speak up Girl
When you think you are cladly Jeer and Denunciation,
Your voice can swap the world
Your voice can change the attitude of world
It's equitable and uneering time to,
Speak up Girl.

# <u>Silence Of A Girl</u>

Sometimes she wants to Weep
Tears try to come in
But remains Upto her Eyes.
Sometimes she wants to Utter
Words try to come in
But residue upto her mouth.
Sometimes she wants to Reveal
Intramural emotions try to come in
But cramped within her Heart.
Sometimes she wants to Broach
Queer thoughts do come in
But just confined upto her Mind.
Sometimes she wants to Relish
Bliss and Elevation do come in
But limited within her Soul.
Sometimes she wants to Eliminate
Grief and sorrows do come in
But bounded within her Misfortune.
And what actually comes
Out is her Silence, Inner deep Silence.

# Giulia Sarro

Her name is Giulia, she's a soul roaming around on this planet. I started writing poetry after having had a sudden spark of inspiration coming from the divine while I was quietly reading on the couch. It didn't make sense at the beginning but she has always loved writing so she didn't question it. So here she is, writing about life, spirituality and untranslatable words.

Dear,
Let your tears water the garden
From where flowers and trees will grow
Every day, some will die and some will bloom
That's part of life
It's a cycle
Learn to feel and to let go
Learn to stand up and to shine
You are a masterpiece.

A new person emerging from the hurt and pain
Coming up from the depth of the ocean
Roses blooming from your scars
Pain dissolving from the skin into the ground
Feel it, let it go, be reborn
You are stronger than ever.

# Garima Pandey

I am Garima Pandey from Jajpur,Odisha. I am 17 years old. I always  believe in Hardwork. I am in 12th standard. My hobbies are Dancing, Reading books, Drawing.

# <u>Struggle Of Rape Victims</u>

I WILL NEVER UNDERSTAND WHY IT IS MORE SHAMEFUL TO BE RAPED THEN TO BE A RAPIST''
When someone is a victim of sexual violence , it affects not only the victims , but also all of the people around them. Sexual violence can affect many people in a victim life: parents, friends, partners, children , co-worker. This point can be very difficult to allow the victims to make his or her own decisions , it can be very tempting to "take over" for a while in an attempt to help the victim deal with the rape. It is important to remember that because of the rape, the survivor felt a loss of control over their life. Re-establishing that control is very important .Try to defer to a survivor's decision, even if they decide to let you make some decision. Then at least that was their choice and not your. If a victim wants to talk, try to be an open listener .If they prefer not to talk about the assault then try to be supportive in other ways, letting them know that you care about him/her and are a willing listener, who acknowledges the feeling of a person , makes a significant positive impact . Sometimes it's very useful to simply be with a person and create a safe-silence. Non-judgmental support helps survivors tremendously as they recover from this traumatic event. Making a police report after a sexual assault can be a very difficult decision for victim. Uncertainty about reporting the assault is common, especially if you know the person who assaulted you . Filling a police report is the first step in beginning the criminal justice process. Many people find it hard to disclose to their parents, but ultimately find parents but love and support helpful to their healing process. Some victims may be concerned about hurting their parents or fear that their family may blame them for the assault. Only the victim can decide if and when to tell their family. When someone you know is sexually assaulted ,it can be a

frightening and confusing time for them and for you :Remember that the person who has been sexually assaulted needs to obtain medical assistance , feel safe ,be believed, know she or he was not at fault , take control of his or her life. There is not one "Right "way to deal with sexual violence; each person has to make his or her own decision. The most common reason many people choose not to tell anyone about sexual assault is the fear that the listener won't belive them. People rarely lie about sexual assault; in fact victims are much more likely to downplay the violence against them. The world today is changing, but unfortunately, sexual assault is still happening every single day. People are beginning to talk about it more but it is still not reaching a point where there is a solution. Sexual violence poses an obstacle to peace and security. It impedes women from participating in peace and domestic processes and in post-conflict reconstruction and reconciliation. As a tool of war it can became a way of life: once entrenched in the fabric of society, it lingers long after the guns have fallen silent .Many Women lose their health, livelihoods, husband ,families and supports network as a result of rape. This in turn, can shatter the structures that anchor community values , and with that disrupt their transmission to future generation children accustomed to acts of rape can grow into adults who accept such acts as the norm .This vicious cycle must stop, as we cannot accept a selective zero-tolerance policy."

TO FELLOW SURVIVORS OF SEXUAL ASSAULT: I DON'T KNOW YOU, BUT I'M WITH YOU.

# Hafsa Amin

Hafsa Amin is a student of 10th standard. She had her initial school at Hamdard Grammar School and Solace International school. She has been writing since she was in 8th standard. Reading about Anne Frank triggered her to drain her emotions on a piece of paper, as Anne said paper has more patience than people, she took that seriously and started writing. She uses "ح" as her pen name as it is the initial of her name (in urdu).

# <u>There Was No Me For Me</u>

Come sit next to me,
Tell me what treasures,
Your broken heart contains,
Tell me how,
your heart was ripped,
and then you were nothing,
More than a heartless person,
We'll talk about your deep,
Ocean eyes,
That reflect your dark memories,
Tell me the tale of your disintegration,
Give me all the charge,
You have been carrying,
From ages,
As I, am the one who is listening,
the cries of your heart,
As my heart too cried,
And there was no me for me.
(Nothing more than dust now)
-From a rape victim to a rape victim.

# **<u>The Story Of Our Separation</u>**

Oh thy mother!
Today I am here to tell you the story,
The story, which I want the world to know,
The story that clearly shows the barbarity of your world.
The story of our separation.
Mother, my soul was innocent and pure!
Neither I hated anyone or teased them more.
I was just eight,
When those monsters made you wait,
I was crying loud when those monsters came,
They scraped my soul without any shame.
Their I was lying, crying with pain,
But no one listened, that was all in vain,
They did that to satisfy their lust,
I don't believe in humanity, not even Him I trust,
After they satisfied their lust, they killed me mother,
There was no fear of god, I could clearly see in their eyes
mother,
Mother, I want justice, and for that they must be killed,
For you know there is pain and anger with which my soul is
filled.

# Himanshi Yadav

A lady from Rajasthan, making her words to be in a wide range. As she being in love with words whole life, joined the writing field in 2009. And became miss poet in school time since graduating. Intrigued with spinning records, and making people to read it. She further mastered this skill and able to bind words with situation. In 2020 a local youtube poetry competition, which consists of a local poem lover person. She gave her write-up in one more book"vazood- eh- zindagi". Himanshi was motivated to further her writing career and went on to make her name for herself in the writing world in order to pursue her passion.

I was captured, no possible way to escape. Wondering if I deserved it, if it was truly my fate. I tried to fly away, but my wings were broken. I was like an innocent cow that he used to prod and poke. My mind filled with confusion, and his filled with lust. He took another part of me with each and every thrust. Tears like elegant pearls gracefully danced down my face. I peered into his soul with a firm look of disgrace. His cold touch was like a vacuum, sucking out the life in me. His ears were wide open, but he wouldn't hear my plea. Standing there in the night, so scared, so exposed. I was covered by a veil of darkness, like satin petals of a rose. The glowing moon looked down at me, peeking through a massive blanket of stars. I could touch it; it seemed so close, but it was really oh so far. Worse than at the doctor; he injected me with filth and dirt. His intention was deliberate; it was very clear and overt. It is a bit funny that a piece of scum is all he'll ever be.

# Heena Farooq

Heena Farooq hailing from Manchowa Budgam.Heen is her pen name. She's currently studying in class 10th in ALamdar mission secondary School Manchowa .In class 7th, she was inspired by her teacher Javeed Moja who writes poems of his own but at that time She was unable to put her feelings in poetic form.She started writing in class 9th.In the beginning it was just to relieve stress. But later it became her passion. She usually writes urdu poetry. The reason behind all this is the loss of her brother and getting separated from her loved.She's a self taught writer.
Email:heenafarooq197@gmail.com
Insta: heenaaaaa08

# <u>Let's Bring A Revolution In Society</u>

A girl was sent as a blessing to her family. But everyone here in the world treated her like a tissue which they used and threw out. She was made to be an angel to fly high and reach heights of success. But we cut her wings and stopped her from dreaming big dreams. Nowadays girls are asked to bend their eyes down while walking on the road Or in the market. To some extent they are right but why don't they teach their boys to respect each and every girl? Girls are being tortured by their in-laws for dowry, They are being molested, Harassed, Raped and then everyone says she was willing to do so which is totally disgusting. Boys are allowed to marry the one they love but girls are considered as characterless even if she thinks so.Instead of all this we should bring a revolution in our society. Let's support her, respect her, and give her a right place for which she has been made by the Almighty.

## <u>Tera Kya Bigada Tha</u>

Ye duniya ka dastoor mujhe samaj mai kyu nahi aaya.
Har ladki ko buri nazar se kyu dekha gaya.
Usko b tou apne baap ne naazu se pala tha.
Aakhir us be gunah ne tera kya bigada tha.
Apni behan ko rehmat aur us begunah ko khilona ku samjha.
Aye darinde kis tarah se woh nazar milaye gi samaaj se mujhe ye samjha.
Kyu bigadi uss maasoom k chehre ki hasi tu ye bata.
Kya uske cheekh ne p tujhe zara sa taras na aaya ye bata.

# Hafsa Khursheed

Myself HAFSA KHURSHEED From jammu and kashmir . I am a student of class 9th and taking education from & DELHI PUBLIC SCHOOL, JAMMU . I am 14 years old. My interest in writing started at a young age. I enjoyed it since I first learned to do it, but my passion really ignited when I was 13 years old. With writing I could create my own world, make up something interesting that happened. There could be good too, and I liked not knowing what happened, but I liked to make my own even better. So I wrote and dreamed of being a best author of picture books and many more. Those years for me weren't easy and I found myself struggling to keep up with writing. I always tried to give my best towards writing. First I started from an essay contest. So, I read the novel and submitted an essay. The essay was my best work and impressive. I had written in a while, but I wrote. It was the first step back into writing. I can never give up writing, no matter how hard I try and, for it's an addiction, that is too pretty good.

# <u>The Real Girago</u>

We can't understand the seriousness of this word "rape" even if we try to. The pain of this word can't be felt, the scars it lefts on the victims is really tough to understand and as We know there are many common myths about rape, sexual violence that can cause shame,guilt ,self blame. All girls are just becoming puppet of those boys and mens .We can just give a speech on "rape" , but what about it's victims? the people who fight with the society everyday and are blamed for that thing everyday which isn't even done by them and they are already fighting with themselves.

We live in a society where a "rapist" is considered as a powerful person but the "victim" is considered as a "bad dirty woman". We are basically living in a society which ruins you instead of helping you. Which plays an opposite role in every crime.

"Victims should be referred as the strongest persons,fighters, the real superwomens"!

" We girls are more powerful than the boys "

But NO! we are taught to hate them, see them not as fighters, but as the persons who aren't allowed to get married again, who aren't allowed to live a happy life like others do, who are forced to kill themselves, who are pushed towards depression , and when finally the thing, they did, results into taking their life away,then our society mourns! Come on'. What if they are rape victims,they are beautiful souls, the strongest souls!

And as per our religion NO ONE, means NO ONE has the right to abuse them or hate them!

As i said:

"Victims should be referred as the strongest persons,fighters, the real superwomens"!

# Ilsa Shafi

Hey, it's Ilsa Shafi from Baramulla district Of this mystic valley of hidden pain-painters.In the growing and glowing time of this tough life, I saw myself getting indulged in the universe of writing and hiding it somewhere in my room. But after getting to know what actual talent is meant for, I started to show my write-ups to my "one and only mentor"- my dad, who used to add wonders in my childish poems.Even being only 17, I feel grateful to possess a talent that defines how deep I can go in someone's pain and turn it into beautiful poetry.Whatever I write or whatever I make people read, is just to show how beautiful words can be and how alluringly one can play with them.I hope to see a positive change in people, especially my Kashmiri mates to pick up their pens and start making their names as renowned as Mehjoor.

# <u>Soul So Cold</u>

My soul is so cold that:
every inch of the belief is crushed,
So with every word I say,
My mouth shuts me up.
Just because of the actions,
Those actions,
that made my goodness just fall away.
My soul is so cold that;
Now I don't even seek pardons anymore.

# <u>The Becoming</u>

O' those who took the aura away,
She ain't devastated as you sway.
Crying never made her weak
Rather, reformed her scars bleak.
Maybe changed got the way she was,
Now busy loving only her flaws.
"A big crazy" may the world call,
As if it will make her trip to fall.
Nothing would cease, it's just the coming,
A return of the Junoesque- the becoming.

# <u>The Mirror Of Shame</u>

The sighs that will reign thy life,
And will reign their hearts alike.
The demon that welcomed gates for them,
So many gates to taste the hell.
Thy regret won't ever let them sleep
The cries of victim's shout and weep.
Even if they won't ever take the blame
Covertly will be sinking in the mirror of shame.

# Ishrat Ashraf

Ishrat Ashraf hails from panzinara shaltang Srinagar.Recently completed Bachelor's degree from Govt. Women's College Nawakadal. She is a social activist ,islamic tutor, writer,painter, motivational speaker and works on rights and status of women.
Gmail:ishratashraf212@gmail.com
Instagram:_ishrat_ashraf

# <u>Women De - Womanized</u>

The word is saturated with propaganda touring the "sustained development and empowerment of women". Leaders from around the world and human rights activists have joined the campaign calling for gender equality and the liberation of women . This movement is so against this new culture crusade. Streets have become the center of activities ,restaurants and parks have become the places of romantic ventures. Morality has been completely ignored by the protagonists of reform. Robbers enjoy prosperity, gangsters protected by politicians and judges ,homosexuality flourishes.Women who opt to rear and educate children are regarded as ignorant and oppressed whilst nudity and promiscuity are branded as liberation. Morals dwindle,manners deteriorate ,corruption increases and vulgarity has become the order of the lady .Is this the virilization we meant to emulate? In Islam ,the rights and responsibilities of women are equal to those of the male but not necessarily identical. Equality and identity are distinct from each other .This distinction is of permanent importance. Equality is desirable, just and fair ,identity is not .People are not created identical but they are created equal. In Islam ,the role of man and women is complimentary and cooperative rather than competitive. The journalist, Dorothy Thomson very aptly states that,"women put precisely on the same level as man has been de-womanized ".

The empowerment of women is aimed at destroying the traditional family as we know it today. It wants to alternate their responsibilities concerning housework and demands appropriate measures to improve women's ability to earn income beyond traditional occupations.A natural  natural duties demands so much time and absorption that opting for a career outside the home would naturally damage the primary role of building human society. The fact is that ,nature itself

has divided human activities into three parts .Preservation, procreation and education of human hall,as opposed to sincerity ,stability and the acquisition of human needs.The first duty is assigned to women ,which is the keeping with their physique just as men have been granted a physical keeping with their physique just as men have been granted a physical keeping with their natural duties. If primary processes of life,which are based on biological facts are ignored, time will have its revenge.... Once cannot assault nature with impurity. Islam neither suggests that women should be excluded from a social life nor dose deprive them of the benefits of communal life of the community. It invites their natural cooperation in all fields of life ,but only within the code of conduct prescribed for them by them by the Shariah .The Holy Quran states:
"The believers, men and women are protectors and friends of each other.They enjoy what is just and forbid what is evil, they observe regular prayers and practice regular charity and obey Allah and his Messengers' '. (Surah Al Taubah,79)
This verse invites the cooperation of Muslims, men and women in all maters ,spiritualcan only  well as material and is the basic of the organizational and functional set up of a Muslim society. According to this verse ,men and women are indispensable partners of life and without their active participation and cooperation, society can not achieve any real and durable progress. Prophet Mohammad (PBUH) said:
" Women are but the only other half (Shariq) of men " .But this does not mean that full participation can only be achieved by men and women who work together, more together in assemblies and mix together as parties. Immurt as a woman obviously is upto  her shoulder .In the business of life and its multiplication, let it be said openly and unequivalently  that all those who teach her that any other business is her business and who in the face of the dilemma of modern problem.

# Jasmine Panda

Miss Jasmine Panda is presently pursuing Ph.D. Chemistry from Ravenshaw University, Odisha, India. She is a Gold Medalist and University Topper in her B.Sc. and M.Sc. She has successfully completed an internship CSIR-SRTP in IICT Hyderabad. She is a Governor's Award winner for YRC. She has received All-Rounder Award in her 12th standard for excellence in extracurricular activities along with studies. She has been a Literary and Cultural Champion in her college days. She has hosted numerous events including International events and has been appreciated as an anchor. Apart from being a versatile orator and debater, she has been a part of 580+ anthologies till now and loves to pen down her feelings! She is an amiable person interested in both Science and Literature, having a wide variety of interests like painting, sketching, acting, anchoring, debating, rangoli making, taking part in extempore, elocution and many more...Publishing her own book someday is something which she aspires....

# Is It Easy To Forget It!

Tightly wrapped up in her black velvet blanket,
Squeezed in a corner surrounded by her toys in her bed,
Disha kept shivering many nights after that night....
Struggling to get back to normal again,
Accepting her ever-cherished life once again,
A conversation started between her heart and mind as usual!
"Forget it, just forget it" her heart said.
"It's not easy, not at all easy", her mind said.
"What has happened was destined to happen", heart said.
"But should no one raise their voice against it?", mind questioned.
"But you have the power to forget... please forget", heart said.
"It's not easy, not at all easy", her mind said.
"Everything will be alright hereafter", my heart consoled.
"But one who should take revenge...", mind argued.
"Revenge! No, I don't want to....", heart sighed.
"You have to my dear....", mind stated.
"Stop it! Just Stop the conversation.....", Disha shouted.
Enough.... Stop it.... Forget it....
Remembering the dark phases she went through in her life,
Sustaining the darkest nights, she had ever experienced...
She cried, "Stop it, it's enough...."
Leave me alone.... please leave me alone, pleaded Disha.
"Try to cope with everyone, behave normal my dear", heart suggested.
"Can you imagine what she's going through?" mind questioned.
"Yes, yes, but time heals everything, try to forget it!" my heart answered silently.
"But my dear, revenge is to be taken and...", my mind argued boldly.
"Stop it I said....! Stop it" Disha cried.
Disha couldn't convince herself to forget it....
And as usual, this was just one more night in Disha's life...
In the invisible trauma, seeking answer from the same confusion,
"Is it really easy to forget it", she asked herself again.

# Krishnaveni

N. Krishnaveni is a Postgraduate in English Literature from the reputed institution of St. Xavier's College. She is an aspiring writer and a budding poet. One of her poems "My Beloved Damsel!" has been published in The Literary Herald journal. She is a co-author of anthologies like "A kiss of love" , "Deep words" , "Pet love". Most of her poems deal with the theme of nature, human emotions, and philosophical thoughts. It is universal in nature. Her poetry voices out the deepest emotions and secrets that are left unspoken and destined to be beautifully inked. Having a creative artistic propaganda, her writings hail from articulate thoughts with coherence, spontaneity  and flowery language.
Gmail veninatarajan24@gmail.com

# A Fighter

She is a princess in reign,
Bunch of scoundrels makes her life ruin.
The disgusted crime makes
All daughters overly afraid.
The whole air taut with a strenuous fear
And fidgety for the evermore despair.
That one night turned her life
Topsy-turvy and a heap of shambolic.
The acute crime of shrewd convict
Becomes a common thing to be heard.
It's a well-planned assault
That receives a shameful manly applause.
Heinous crime and guilt bag full
A wicked wrong deed
Justified by a vicious race for ages indeed.

(1)

Whole world conspires against the victim
Liable to mute her stand all the time.
Little they latched onto
That she is the sea of flames with no doubt.
You flung the debris of shame and insults
But nothing could snatch her virtue and guts.
She is not a slinky model meat
To cater your carnal desire and need.
The time is enough to digest
The society's narrow outlook.
She is not a pathetic survivor
To show up with a posed laughter
Hiding the painful tears behind.
But a mere fighter with a will now
For the whole world has to bow.

# Maheena Zehra

Maheena Zehra, a 19 years old young talented writer and a pen holder, motivational speaker and a poetess and a debater hailing from Hawal area of Jammu and Kashmir.She herself said that she had been writing from almost the time when she was just 11 years old but, her passion for writing turned into profession and ambition some few years back. She writes poems on various issues too and expresses herself through her social media account as she is a blogger too. Although she is a commerce student, she loves writing and sharing her views with the people around her. She shares all her quotes, poems and writings on her social media account and people too abbreviate her works.

Instagram @_maheena_zehra @maheenawrites

Gmail: maheenazehra786@gmail.com

# <u>Dedicated To The Struggles Rape Victims</u>

The topic which itself tells us the whole is " The Rape Victims" when one sits to write on it, the person himself shivers when writing on it. Before going through the rape victims, it is important to write on why this topic needs to be enlightened. Well, we already know about the crimes that occur against women, either it will be domestic violence, suppressing their voice or blaming for every single instance for no fault of there's. Although measures are taken now to give women their rights and to give them what they deserve, they are an important part of the society, giving their right to vote, right to education, etc. But despite all these optimistic steps taken, there are always crimes against women knowing at the door and one crime against women is rape. A serious threat to the dignity of the women and an assault on their morals, their safety. Though we know that rape is the establishment of sexual relations with a women, against her will, forcibly done but the story doesn't end here because rapes even happen with a married lady done by her husband, when she isn't willing to have sexual relations. The cause of this immoral and unethical act is definitely the male lust. When a man loses his dignity, he commits this immoral act. It is such a sin for which even God will refuse to forgive. The time a man sees a lady with lustful eyes, sees her as an entity/a thing or a commodity meant to fulfill his desires, it is the time he loses his whole existence because it fails to commemorate he also has a mother, a wife and may have a daughter. This is in fact the greatest irony ever through which one comes across. Though we know the outcomes of this immoral act but, the rape victims i.e; women suffer for the whole of their life because of it. The rape victims i.e; women lose their psychology balance and even, some fail to recognise themselves and some get jerks and some even get traumatized because of this immoral act. The post-rape physiological imbalances are obvious and even, in most of the cases, the victim pushes itself to the edge of perishing its life. Rape Victims don't need sympathy only they need family support, support from the

society and the friends so that she may develop enough intrinsic as well as extrinsic strength to fight for her justice and for the punishment of the culprit. In most of the cases, either the rape victim don't get the necessary requirement support from the people around or her voice is suppressed due to the fear of society, what the society will think, etc. But, these are mere unsupportable and unjustified excuses because if the rape victims don't come forward for her justice, then its the whole society which fails because today she were the victim of the immoral act and tomorrow it can be any other person, you or me or anyone. Such men really don't deserve to live among us and they should be given penalty for their sin.We sadly remember the horrific incident of mass rape of Kashmiri women in Kunan and Poshpora villages that happened in February 23, 1991, although the case was reopened after a long time in 2011 when a petition was filed by some social activists from Kashmir who wanted to remove the dust of fear and hopelessness from the victims. After a long and difficult process the Jammu and Kashmir High Court directed the state government to pay compensation to those affected.The state government initially agreed, but then changed its mind, and challenged the High Court's decision in the Supreme Court of India, where the case is still being heard.In Kashmir most officials seem to speak in what sound like cautious parables. But, as I earlier said "YOU HAVE TO DO IT YOURSELF"

Although, there are strict measures that have been taken against the male genre who commit this sin and to reduce the rape cases as much as possible like, Aasiya, an 8 years old girl of a nomadic tribe from Kathua area of Jammu region was given justice, though belated but, the culprits received their penalty.

As a society, we it's also our responsibility to help the victims of rape or to ensure measures inorder to reduce the probability of these acts. But, since what had been done can't be corrected,

# **Mohsin Bhat**

 I am Mohsin from district bandipora kashmir. I am a lab technology student.
My poet is all about broken hearts. Related many topics.

Ek ladki ab farmaish si huvi hei
Her baazaru mei numaish si huvi hei
Chalay they vo seedhay saadhay ban kar
Her wehshiyat ab un p zahir si huvi hei.


Gaaray ka ghr ujda chanan aur vo andheeri raat
Kaagaz aur qalum utha kar likh dil ki baat
Vo zoor zaar baarish vo meray aansu aur dil k halaat
Bayaan kar beitha me kaawaz p us din apnay saaray raaz


Us raaz ki baat na kar
Aysi koi gustaakh na kar
Manzil tay hei taqdeer mei
Phr chalta ja ruknay ki baat ba jar

# Mir Mohammed Adnan

Mir Mohammad Adnan Hails from Bumhama Kupwara. An Engineering Student Born in 1998. He is an amateur writer and passionate story teller.He loves advocating social harmony & campaigning social enthusiasm to reach out vulnerable sections of our society. "An enthusiastic who aim to learn things within the developments in the society & then love to address the same things simultaneously " Dedicating his first blog to those victims who are actual warriors of life who lost everything in this world of beasts still put beautiful smile and have courage to live on this life ,The real superheros known as rape victims. A short stanza for those beautiful souls who became victims of beasts . My image was blurred in your cigarette smoke. I will still rise and ask for a just revoke..

Mir Mohammad Adnan
{Insta}  adnan_ujdi_riyasat

# <u>Maire – Dastaan</u>

Mai hui thi kissi janwar kai hawas ki shikaar.
koie na tha insan wahan jo sunta meri cheek _o_pukaar .
Dhar Dhar mein khati rhi thokrei jab dhondhnai nikli insaaf.
Jo dekh chukai thai manzar wahn woh b kr gyai inkaar .
Na ja skhi mein ghar, na mein ja skhi bazaar.
Agar shakas tha ek batien hui hazaar .
Kaat khanai ko atai thai ab dar _o_dewaar.
sabar sai ab rooh b honai lgi thi bemaar.
Ye mana ki ADAM khata kar kai b tha sheh-sawar .
Kya hawa ki Aabiru ka nahi tha koie waqar.
Gayai har kisi kai pass jisai tha phlai sar-o-kaar.
Magar Fakt koie na sun paya meri cheek-o pukaar.
Koi na tha insaan wahan jo sunta maire cheek-o-pukaar.

# Misbah Mehraj

Misbah, a 2005 born.From the town of mountains Baramulla, kashmir.She is a writer and poetry is her thing.It's just like when she isn't able to express her sentiments,It comes on a page in the form of a poetry.If she isn't found spending time with family,You will either find her on her desk or with the football.Yeah these are her priorities and she loves them.

# Rape, The Unseen Act

She still remembers that awful day,
When the devil came and took off her wings,
Didn't knew what was happening,
As she was a mere soul.
But Now she knows everything,
Those hidden scars on her body,
Painful screams and pleads remain silent under the pallor of
pain,Streaming tears like a stream
remained hidden behind her eyes,
Slippery Slithering movement of pain,
Still lives inside her.
Sun rise,Sun Shine!
But she always lived in sunset,
Became an Opacarophile.
And wrecked her life.
But now the sun will rise with a hope,
Shine with the success,
And she, She will rise n shine with the sun,
A Solist,
With a beautiful spirit.

# <u>Turn The Aconite Into Violet</u>

People saying' You are deficient,
Characterless,and much more...
But my dear daffodils,
All you are is a woman,
A woman you own to be.
Remember what you must do,
When they think,
Your generosity is your fragility,
Make you subordinate to a man,
Like a tiger and a mouse.
Just speak up,
Speak up for your own self ,
Speak up the unspoken words,
What are you waiting for?
Don't behave like a raven,
Awaken the sleeping dragon,
Rise the fallen fighter,
Burn the extinguished fire in you,
In the time of wind,
Be like the storm,
You are a real warrior,
You are the real superhero,
Life exists in you,
And ends in you,
Just speak up for yourself.

# Mohammad Akram

I was born and brought up in the countryside of district Baramulla and had my early education from my native village. I shifted to the main town Baramulla for secondary studies and used to put up with my Maasi. I had a flavour for writing poetry from the age of 14 (class 9). However, I did not pay too much attention to my writings due to pressure from higher education.

I became a teacher, after spending some years in research and other activities. After getting a job, I got some time to write and would spend on writing Urdu, Kashmiri poetry, and English prose, mostly humorous, and critical to social happenings.
This year, I have been honoured and adjudicated as a Promising Young Poet by JKAACL and participated in All India Urdu Mushaira at Jammu.

# ओर कब तक

जिस की आस हे तैरै दर से,
कयुँ इतना अब ड़रती हे।
युँ तो खास हे तैरै घर से,
कयुँ इतना अब ड़रतो हे।

जिस नै तुम को खून से सींचा,
उस का तुमनै खून किया।
ऐ बेदरदा तैरै शर से,
कयुँ अब इतना ड़रती हे।

तुम ने वहशी पन से उसकै,
फूल से तन मन को रूनदा।
वो तेरी सोहबत के हश्र से,
कयुँ अब इतना ड़रती हे।

अनधे हो कया, दिखता नहीं हे,
यह लढ़की कुच साला हे।
मासूमी भी तेरी नज़र से,
कयुँ अब इतना ड़रती हे।

यह तो माँ हे, या फिर आपा,
या हे बीवी या बेटी।
ऐसै रिशतूँ की चक्कर से,
कयूँ अब इतना ड़रती हे।

कितने शूपयां, कितने कुठवा,
कितने हथरस हे बाकी।
ज़नदगानी की ज़रबो कसर से,

कयूँ अब इतना ड़रती हे।

कया मज़हब ने नहीं कहा हे,
यह देवी हे, पाक बोहत।
फिर मज़हब के ऊलटे असर से,
कयूँ अब इतना ड़रती हे।

चूपी सादी अक्रम तू भी,
गुनाह का हिससा बन भेठा।
नारूँ की आवाज़ि बेहर से,
कयूँ अब इतने ड़रती हे।

# Maleeha Sofi

Maleeha Sofi is a student of Journalism aiming to become a professional writer and a journalist in future. She started writing two years back. She writes motivational content and wants to get into public speaking. She interacts with people to know more about prevailing problems and try to give their solutions through her words.

# A Death Long Before It's Funeral

"Good Morning!  Students, I am highly obliged to address you on the beautiful eve of Women's Day. I wish all the pretty ladies over here a very Happy Women's Day. At present times, more than wishing you a happy women's day, I would like to wish you a safe women's day Or probably a safe life. Women are deprived of basic rights, they are ill treated and also there is an increase in crimes against women. We would definitely not want to continue this in future. I want every male present here to take a pledge that we will ensure the deserved respect and safety to women. We can do so by providing it to the women around us first and eventually women all around will find peace in a friendly atmosphere. I won't take much of your time today. I would actually like it if you will enjoy your day. Thank you for hearing my words. Enjoy lovely ladies".

Claps were echoing all around the school auditorium as the vice - principal's speech came to an end. He stepped down the podium. He was soon gathered by some of his colleagues. " What a speech Iqbal Sir! " , " You outshined the event " , commented those colleagues. His speech was loved by all. As the school function continued, there were many programs going on. Some skits and some speeches in favor of women were so beautifully executed that all the students were full of enthusiasm. After all the performances, students were tired and the conclusion was announced. All the students who participated in performances headed to a room where all the necessary stuff regarding their parts in the event was kept. All the students reached the room and packed their belongings. As a norm, a group of girls started talking about other students and teachers. It was a group of 5 girls Sameena, Iqra, Zainab, Yusra and Urwa. They studied in 5th standard. Almost all were about 10-11 years of age.

Sameena : The skit presented by 8th class students was so good friends. I felt every part of it so well.

Urwa: Yes, you are right but what can you people say about Iqbal Sir's speech? He was smiling all the time. I never thought he is

this much soft spoken. I came to know his reality and that's so beautiful, so, my favorite part was his speech.

Yusra: I agree with Urwa on this note. I mean that was just a skit. They were acting after all. But Iqbal Sir put all his emotions into his speech. He was today's rockstar.

Zainab: Will you stop it friends? How can you say the students in the skit were just acting? Yes, they were acting but how well they acted that we all felt it. You can't ignore that they presented the skit really well.

Iqra: ( Smiling) If your important discussion is over, could you people bother to look around. Everyone has left. Now move fast.

Rest of the 4 girls sighed and packed their bags. All those moved out of the room. On reaching some distance, Iqra realised that she had left some of her books in the room. She told her friends about it but they were still in their discussion of who performed better. Iqra thought that she will return in the time they will feel her absence. She turned back and rushed to the room.  As she entered the room she couldn't find her books there. She checked for the book under the tables, on the window shelves and here and there but didn't get any clue. Soon, she heard some noise as that of tables colliding with each other coming from the next room. She went to see as no one was supposed to be there. As she entered the room, she saw the school keeping maid, Zahida, was cleaning the room. Zahida was called by the name Aaya Maa by all the students. Zahida was loved and respected by students for her kind nature. Iqra greeted Zahida and said, " Why are you still here"? " If I don't stay here to do this, who will make your class worth sitting for you, my dear child "? , replied Zahida with a grin. They both exchanged a smile but both conveyed different meanings. Zahida smiled to show her love to the concern of Iqra and Iqra smiled to show the respect for the dedication Zahida has for her work.

# Misbah Dar

Talking about Misbah  Dar ,the first thing I would like to say is her helping nature . I have seen her multiple times helping the needy one with bundles of love for others. She is a very sensible , sensitive and suave hearted person . I have never seen flocinocihiliphilification and agathokakological  her in . And last but not least I would say her wetting skills always impresses me becoz everyone can relate with her words.

Urna tha usko sab se auncha shyad tabhi be-vaja usko milti thi saza.

Ghut kr jeeney vali zindagi usko gavara na thi.

Shayad tabhi ab vo be huda kehlaney lagi.

Zindagi mein nafrat k ilava usko sab ataa tha,

Shyad tabhi ab usko koi hosla na dena chahta tha.

Saval to uskey bhi hazaar they shyad yahi vaja hai k sab usko samajtey bekar they.

Har din, had mint, har second usk sath hoti thi na-insafi aur jab vo mangti thi insaf to kr di jati thi uski baizti.

Gandi nazrey tumhari hoti hai pr saar juka kr usko chalna parta hai.

Chalo man letey hai vo tum se kamzore hai,

Par 9 mahiney apni koke mein rakh kr akhir mein tumhey janam deti bhi vo hai.

Hamesha gunnah krney k bad tum kehtey ho galti tumhari nhi usk libas thi,

Tou btao kya kumi thi uss 8 saal ki asifa k libas mein,

Tou btao kya kumi thi uss 2 saal ki twinkle sharma k libas mein,

Tou ye btao kya kumi thi uss 6 mahiney ki masoom si bachi k libas mein,

Kumi usk libas mein nhi kumi tum mein hai,

Galti usk libas ki nhi galti tumhari gandi soch ki hai.

Kon kehta hai k urney k liye pankh zaroori hai,

Kon kehta hai k uski qamyabi k liye uska lrka hona zaroori hai.

Zada kuch nhi par ek sawal to mera bhi hai k kon kehta hai k vo larki hai isiliye ussey khul kr jeeney ka haq nhi hai..

# Qurat Ul Ain

Qurat-ul-ain,
A young girl from Baramulla Kashmir is passionate about penning down her thoughts. She writes about all the forms of joys and sufferings that we humans go through out life. She had earlier worked in the anthology book "ALFAAZ, THE POWER OF WORDS", and has got her debut book "INTIMACY AND THE SCARS TACIT" published out recently, which is getting a decent enough response from the people.
Now, here she choose to take the stand of the rape victims and wanted to wake up the people through her words.
Instagram @_qurat.ulain

# <u>Things She'll Never Speak</u>

Her tears have acid, that fall off her eyes and stream down
her face,
Would you follow their track, you got the change just in
case?
She cries in dark corners, her world looks bleak,
her eyes hold the stories, she's too afraid to speak.
The story of her past,
of anger of pain,
she might seem okay,
don't get fooled, just look again.
The scars under her clothes,
that bleed without a halt,
Go around and tell her,
Pain isn't always her fault.
The grazes on her skin, scream out loud,
the names of the places, where she couldn't even shout.
Looking at the sky, she curse her fate,
she believed in love, it's you who made her hate.
Those inhumane things, that made her fall,
Go look her in the eyes, you'll see it all.

# <u>Scary World</u>

Why are you standing there?
What are you thinking of?
You don't need to fear them, tell me who they are?
They shock your breath, now they shake your soul,
and you're taking up everything, thinking you'd never feel
whole.
A pretty girl with a smile, turned to a pale cold night,
Don't let them conquer you, the eyes that crumble you might.
It's never you, nor your body, the reason of this pain,
but their ill thoughts and venom in the sight, that let you to vain.
The deliberate touches while walking through a crowd,
they'll say it's narrow, no matter how much space they've found.
Those awkward stares, from head to toe,
leaving a scar on your mind, wherever you go.
Commenting on your body, thinking it as bravery of men,
I guess they even made an alone girl feel safe,
but oh! I don't remember when?
Following you on your way, that moment wreck souls,
and girl, if they got the chance, you'll be left for a lifetime in
holes.
Your parents aren't supposed to walk with their head up, Ah!
the society of norms.
Feels so unworthy to live, in all the forms.
But sssshhhh!
You can't speak with your pitch high,
you'll be titled a bitch, a slut, a hoe,
even your friends won't stand for you, against is not always a
foe.
They've lost their conscience and you're losing yourself,
the taunts of the society, that is what isn't letting you stand.
The world may ask you why you pay attention to these things?

But let me ask you, "Why not to?"
Sweetheart, they don't own you.

# Ranivah Khursheed

This is Ranivah khurshid sodagar from Shopian
 A bidding poetry writer, co-author & a student
I started writing from the age of 15.
I always try to pen down the pain of my society, my writings
are for those who can't speak for themselves.
Writing is the best way to convey our thoughts and messages
to everyone and I feel proud that I have the art of writing.
According to me a pen and some sheets of papers are the most
powerful weapons that can bring a revolution.
Writing is the best way to motivate and inspire people around
us and I always try to do the same.
Allhamdullilah for the beautiful beginning of writing.

A dark Stormy night
A dark Stormy night and unheard cries
Suffocation of blameless heart
Uncountable screams, unpleasant touches
Yes! My burning heart again calls the name NIRBHAYA
oh! Angel how did you bear, four lusty criminals
Your body were brimming with scares
Oh! Just stop them by trembling hands
Stop the demons
Pain and bleed spots ruined your life
Your father were waiting your mother were yelling
You were bearing the never ending pain
Your frame lost the battle
Didn't you go back oh! Angel
Didn't you go back

# <u>Rape Under The Spacious Sky</u>

It was that strange hour of my life
When some ferocious men raped me
Under the spacious sky
I too had a dream that lasts forever
But those are being indulged and pampered
With the torment of my heart
Oh Almighty! Is there any communication?
Through which i convey my entreaty to you
My optimistic body feels sprained
Behind the walls of some wrenched life
What is this frenzied and unrestrained behavior?
That spoils a women within a second
Where should i go with this brutal anguish?
Tell me oh the healer of my Twenty shades
My breaths become now vanished
And my heart rate becomes my yearning from death.

# Roonaq Fayaz

I'm Roonaq Fayaz from Kanli bagh baramulla. I'm a student of class 11th in Med + Non med stream. I wanna conquer the world with my knowledge. I started writing in lockdown.I found Dawning dusk (for the struggle of Rape victims) the best book to get published for the first time. Inshaallah I'm gonna continue writing as long as I have competency to speak the truth.

E-mail: jaaniram12@gmail.com

# A Sobbing Dad

Hey Beautiful, why are you so blue
Is there anything happened to you
Loved one tell me, I will hear
I'll try to wipe your tear
I'm your father, I will understand
I know with my support, you will withstand
There is nothing hidden from me
You have been raped,look I can see
I wanna know , don't feel shy to say
I'm myself moribund, my sheen fay
Don't lose hope, please choose life
I still love you and my respect for you is rife
Please don't leave me like my spouse
There is no one to run our house
I have a dream to tie you to your love
Tell me whom you loved, my enchanting dove
Look I'm crying, how could you see me sobbing
Wake up, let's go back home stop my heart from throbbing
Come dear let's teach your culprit a lesson
He is a hound, let's take the right from him to live as a person
Let's go, I know you are strong
Roll up , we have to prove him wrong.
You are my love , please don't let me cry
You are brave , without justice how can you bid me bye.

# <u>A Sin</u>

When a girl is raped, not only She is raped
But a family is raped, her father , her mother, her self respect
and their entire life is raped.
Her dreams are raped.Her life is ruined.
She is deprived of  happiness.
She becomes a living corpse .Her life is a hell,
Her demise is a scar upon the heart of her family.
A women is a word of few letters
But She is enough to light the whole world
A girl is a word of few letters
But She endures every impossible ache
A lady is a simple word of few letters
But She alone can change the world
Adorning herself is not sin
Loving herself is not a sin
Caring for herself is not a sin
But yeah!
Your awful gaze on her is a sin
Your worst intention is a sin
Your bad verdict is a sin.

# Sundus Rasheed

I'm Sundus Rashid from Baramulla, Kashmir. I'm a student of class 11th . I began to write poems in 2016. I wrote my first poem on my motherland, Kashmir ,under the title" Kashmir In Crisis". I'm going to publish my first book named after her smile.  Here is a collection of poems related to my real life experience or how as a girl I feel and how i take things ,actually about a lot of things which were just prisoned in mind, difficult to talk about but easier to pen down...Most of people can relate these poems as whatever I witnessed or experienced is common nowadays.

# **<u>Restless Soul</u>**

A voice coming from the sky
I am in paradise now
I thought, I would be able to fulfil my desires
But before that I expired
Holding the hand of my parents
Wanted to show my talents
But as I stepped out of my home
They lead me to my grave
People of my own native place
Snatched my soul from me!
No one heard my painful scream
They gave me deep wounds & destroyed my dream
In this beautiful world of your's O'lord!
Which type of judgement is this?
Only you can hear my pain
That's why to you, I complain
Humans exist without humanity they proved
By their lust my pious soul they removed
Some of your people are worse than the devil
Not even once , they thought of my level.

# Sayiba Hilal

She's sayiba hilal, studies in 12th standard, did her schooling from St Joseph's bla. She's ambitious about launching her debut book suisad really very soon,as she has always believed in the power of words, they can break you! they can heal you! Sayiba says,"i had never thought that I would be able to jot down my pain in such way, that it would turn it into fetching poems".Behind every beautiful poem there is always a baggage of unbearable, unuttered, n inexpressible affliction. As, when tongue is not able to utter eyes begin to pour them on paper.

# <u>She Waited For The Day To Dawn</u>

She waited for the day to dawn
So she could play in her lawn;
A girl with bright eyes
Her heart did not hide any lies;
Looking at the flowers to bloom
a part of sunray touched her face when the sky was full of
brume;
Within an hour everything changed
Someone came to her who was so strange;
He said am your friend; taking her to an unknown place
He inappropriately touched her face;
She was innocent
He thought he was an omnipotent;
She screamed,
He covered her face with a cloth
Without knowing she was as delicate as a moth;
He left her bruised
She was so badly abused;
Blood was dripping off her body
This she couldn't tell anybody;
She washed off the blood
Ah! Man! She was a 6 year old little bud;
A monster ruined her,
She kept quiet
She knew she had lost her fight;
she didn't wanted the day to dawn
So she couldn't never play in the lawn.

# Shafaq Qadri

Shafaq hilal qadri from palhallan pattan
Pursuing graduation from pattan degree college
She has  been interested in writing for a long time now. Mostly
writes about love, self dependence , womens.

# <u>She Will Rise With Every Fall</u>

She is left with a blank space
Her soul crushed and razed
She was unleashed layer by layer
Her spirit forced to tremble with fear
Underneath her skin, her heart
Throbbed in pain , was ripped apart
Left in agony with no mercy
She was looted of her innocency
She is disdained by the society
Her pain aggravated very wisely
She wants to shine but only burns
She lurks in darkness and mourns
But she will rise with every fall
Stiffen with taunts big or small
Her beauty will lavish once again
Her flowers will blossom with the end of pain.

# <u>Dard Ki Intihaa</u>

Bedard khamoshi uski zaat bangayi
Ik pal main wo noor badzaat bangayi
Kisi aur k gunahun ka azaala karegi
Khoobsurat subah amawas ki raat bangayi
Har pal main dard ka tazkira hoga
Wo hayat-e-zindagi behayaat bangayi
Uski shaam ki subah jaane kb hogi
Jeeti huii baazi ki wo maat bann gayi.

# Sahil Shakeel

SAHIL SHAKEEL is a promising writer, hailing from District budgam of Jammu and Kashmir state, India. He is 16 years old and has developed the craze of writing since he was 10. With love towards nature divulged in the heart his words scent naturalism,truth being the ink he writes about happiness, positivity, his dejections and romanticism.The writer aspires to be an IAS officer. The writer has faced several downs but withstood as a strong warrior and turned his misery into pearls. Books being his friends and writing poetry a plaything. Sahil Shakeel fancies publishing his own book. Despite his writing skill the writer has shown some competence in academia and has bagged the district quiz competition in 2019.The writer has been a part of various anthologies two of them are NANHE farishtey and The living paradise anthology further Dawning dusk's being his third published work in the form of anthology.

Why
Everything got altered
That eve begot a new life
Abruptly each horizon rampaged
O God! Why I was ravaged
An untainted lass full of joy
Used with wanton with utter toy
Knew nothing of the cruel world
Her chastity was tarnished sans coy
Was returning from the institution
Some wicked men followed with frustration
They were riveting me with impure gaze
Aftermath, I wept as the life was full of maze
They caused scars and envenomed my soul
Each moment I try to heal but I fail
The remembrance of a raging tempest still ail
Numbness on brain but tears still hail
The treacherous eve drowned me at once
I have been left in shambles from thence
The folks slay me as I endeavour to obliviate
That impeded caput never got elated.

# Smriti Suman

Smriti Suman is from the land of Mahavira and Buddha ,Bihar.She is a student. She loves  playing with words and exploring herself. writing is like a sukoon for her. According to her "everyday to me is rather a new exploration rather than just a day.I wish to become a self published writer for society's welfare and yeah the best influencer through my writing".she has participated in many anthologies and newspapers. You can catch her on insta @the_blue_moon_girl

हम रहते हैं एक ऐसे रोगग्रस्त समाज में ।
जहां कोई अस्तित्व नहीं स्त्री का इस समाज में।।
कहीं मां कहीं बहन कही पत्नी के रिश्ते से जानी जाती है।
हर मोड़ पर उसकी पहचान बदलती सी जाती है।।
सिर्फ स्त्री ही पुरुष के नाम से जानी जाती है।
कहीं पिता कहीं पति कहीं पुत्र के नाम से जानी जाती है।।
पति पत्नी होते हैं एक दूजे के पूरक।
क्या सिर्फ पत्नी होती है पति की पूरक?
पति के मृत शरीर के होते ही भस्म।
पत्नी की खुशियां श्रृंगार को भी कर दिया जाता है भस्म।।
पति के भस्म होने के साथ
 एक पत्नी भस्म हो सकती है।।
पर क्यू एक स्त्री को भी कर दिया जाता है भस्म?
क्यों उस पर रीति रिवाज थोपकर? कठपुतली सा छोड़ दिया जाता है?
क्यों हर मोड़ पर उसे अलग-अलग तराजू में तौला जाता है??
क्यों हर मोड़ पर स्त्री करती है यह त्याग??
क्यू पुरुष नहीं दे सकता यह बलिदान??
लाख चलाया हाथ पैर किया विद्रोह इस समाज का।
फिर मैं भी हो गई हिस्सा इसी समाज का।।
अब मेरा भी समाज करेगा निर्माण एक नए रोग ग्रस्त इंसान का।।।।
हर बार की  ही तरह मां का घर आना हुआ ।
हर बार की ही तरह मन मार विसर्जन करने पहुंची।।
रंग बिरंगे श्रृंगार से सजी मां को देख
मन मंत्रमुग्ध हो उठा।
तभी नजर एक लड़की पर जा रुकी
जो हाथ जोड़े खड़ी थी।।
और कुछ लड़के शराब के नशे में धुत उसे घेरे।
मन व्यर्थ में ही विचलित हो उठा।।
बात तो छोटी सी ही थी।
शर्मा जी इस बार भी मूर्ति ही घर लाए थे।

# Taha Gazala

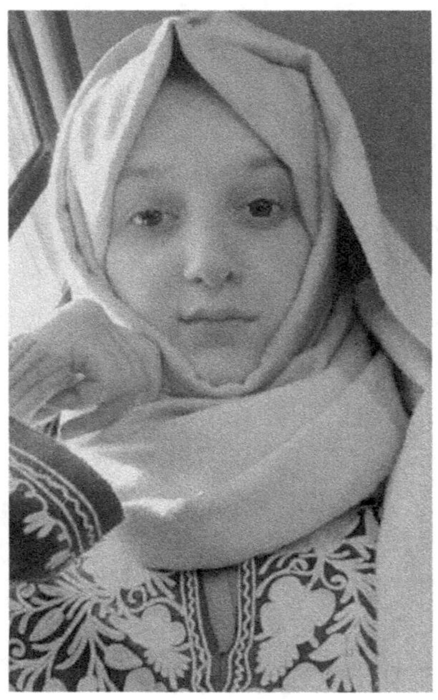

She's taha gazala,a young writer from kashmir .She started writing poetry during her school days.She mostly writes in English and can write in urdu as well.she says,"main reason for showing interest in writing was her own life and her homeland kashmir".Her writing is mainly fictional and some of them are based on her own life.She believes that writing gives her inner peace .she shares a deep connection with her pen,that undoubtedly dissipates gems. Her insta handle is @t.ghazalli

# <u>A No That Changed A Life</u>

I'm forever grateful for this life. I wasn't ready to accept myself after that incident until I met Zaman", said Zuleikha.

Zuleykha, a pretty, intelligent, and ambitious girl lived in Adarsh Nagar, Delhi. Just like any other girl on the planet, Zuleikha too had dreams, dreams of being an IAS officer. She was happy with what she had and wanted to achieve more. Life seemed to be on the right track until life took its turn back.

"I knew I was in peril, so I called for help but there was no one except this group of boys headed by Jafar who were approaching towards me fiercely", said Zuleikha.

Jafar was the son of a politician of that time. He also lived in Adarsh Nagar, Delhi. He had asked Zuleykha for marriage before that incident. Zuleikha wasn't mentally ready for marriage and she wanted to continue her studies. So she said "NO" to Jafar, unaware of the calamity coming her way. Jafar wasn't expecting a "NO" from her because of his misogynistic mentality. The rejection from Zuleikha remained stuck in his mind and he was ready to take its revenge by any means. Even though, if he has a right to ask a girl for marriage, she too has the same right to accept or reject it, but he got engaged in making plans for destroying her life forever.

 Zuleikha was coming back from her college when she was pervaded by this group of boys. She tried to ignore them but there were multiple thoughts tangled in her mind as they started to tease her. Suddenly Jafar blocked her way. Then only she realized that she was in absolute danger and she started to scream for help but all in vain, as the roads were deserted. Jafar forcefully grabbed Zuleykha and his friends tied her hands with ropes. Zuleykha was shrieking and wailing for help when they took her to a forest area but nobody was there to help her. They fainted her with some drugs and for the next half an hour she was unconscious.

As soon as Zuleikha opened her eyes, she saw her torn clothes, and her pretty glorious body turned blue as if someone had beaten her harshly. She tried to stand on her feet but she couldn't. It felt as if all her bones had been crushed and her skin had been ripped off her body. She laid there, sick with shame, too frightened, disgusted, and shocked at what had happened to her. Her body was trembling with pain and heartache that nobody could repair. The last one hour of her life was the most difficult one and it changed her forever. She could see all her dreams shattering in front of her and all her expectations flew away in the air. Zuleikha was completely splintered. She somehow grabbed herself and managed to reach home. Her mother wrapped her in a blanket. Hearing Zuleikha`s cries her father came running out and was shattered after seeing injured Zuleikha in torn-out clothes. It wasn't easy for her to narrate this whole incident in her words. She uttered just two words, "RAPE" and "Jafar". Her parents were shocked. Zuleikha wanted to register a case but her parents denied and her brother beat her instead. She was let down by her family. It was the second most painful thing that ever happened to her. The episode didn't end there, there were still more hurdles in her path. After some days Zuleikha joined college again and thought that she would feel better as nobody knew about the incident. But when she reached college the news had already broken. Nobody was talking to her and everyone treated her as if it was her fault. She then decided to quit her studies as well. Everyone in the society was blaming her for rejecting Jafar's marriage proposal. Months passed, zuleikha was recovering from the pain but the trauma was still there. To come out of the trauma, She tried to go out with her mother veiling her face and body so that nobody could recognize her and one day she was in the market with her mother and suddenly her eyes fell on a beautiful cat lying on the road. She picked the cat up in her lap and started to play with her until zaman asked her to return the cat to him (the cat belonged to zaman). This was the first time when zuleykha met zaman. Zaman fell in love with Zuleikha's beautiful eyes. He noticed that there was something special and attractive in her eyes. Zaman couldn't sleep the whole night, he was completely lost in her thoughts. Without wasting much time

Zaman went to zuleykha`s house with his parents and asked Zuleikha for marriage. Maybe zuleikha`s parents would have said yes but zuleykha immediately said, "NO". Not because she doesn't want to get married but because she thought that zaman and his family didn't know about the incident (zaman and his family were new in the society). Zaman tried to talk to zuleykha but she ignored him. Finally, after some days she was ready to meet him and close the chapter once for all. They finally met at a public park and zuleykha narrated the whole story of that incident.At the end of her conversation, zaman smiled and said, "I know everything that happened to you". Zuleykha was in complete shock and asked Zaman if he knew the story, why would he wish to marry her? Zaman told zuleykha that even if you don't marry me but still I want you to know that it wasn't your fault and that the incident shouldn't be the end of your life but it should be the new beginning. And I would love to be a part of this new beginning. After hearing all this Zuleykha was in a fix what to say but still not sure about the truthfulness of Zaman. After some days Zulaykha said yes and they got married. Life was again on the right track for Zuleikha. She now resumed her degree and was working for her dreams now. She was now happy with what has and loved herself even more now. "I thought life won't be smooth now and I had completely lost myself until zaman made me realize that rape isn't the end of life but it should be the new beginning; a beginning that makes you fall in love with yourself and everything that loves you back," said zuleykha. Well, we can see how a simple "NO" at one point of time and "YES" at another changed zuleykh's whole life. Individual choice is among basic human rights and everybody should be given this right respectfully. Society could have played a good role by not blaming zuleykha for everything that had happened. Rape is a punishable act and anyone refusing this fact is equally punishable. Zuleykha had to go through a lot and all she craved was little care and some extra attention and love.

# Toufeel Chalkoo

Toufeel Rasheed chalkoo  from salamabad uri Jammu and Kashmir. A law student who started his writing during the lockdown. A firm believer of Islam and always try to work according to sunnah.

He wants to express his feelings and thoughts through Poetry. Poetry in itself is a world and he wants to be a part of that world.

# <u>Dil Ki Pukaar</u>

Maine apni izat ko saray aam  bikhartay Dekha
Maine Apne Dil ko roz wa shub sisaktay Dekha
Ye bs magribi tehzeeb ki ek dain ha
Maine khud apni tehzeeb ko ujartay Dekha
Muje  do azeeto ka Malik bna Dala in nay
Ek apna drd aur logoon ki tanqeed ko bhi apnay huq main atay
Dekha
Hum insaaf ke liye kidr ab  Jain gay
Maine apnu ko bhi apnay khilaf khaday hotay Dekha
Hur adalat to yahaan zulam ki Mari ha
Waha bhi sirf intazar hi ko agay badhatay Dekha
 Ek roz ye dour bhi khtm ho jai ga
Maine Hur dour ko atay jatay Dekha
Insaaf to yahaan bht door ki baat ha likn
Sirf apni takleef hi ko hamesha badh jatay Dekha.

# <u>Halay Dil</u>

Ab to lgta ha yahaan bacha Kuch bhi nhi
Hur traf to sirf andehray hi chai Hain
Tandeeq ke bazaar bhi Sur gram Hain unmain bhi sirf hamaray
hi naam aye Hain
Hur kisi ne  huk ko juthlanay main
 Hur kisim ke zoor azmain Hain
Dukh hota ha apni Zindagi pr
Hum kin zalimu main rehnay aye Hain
Asal zalim ko kisi ne Kuch na kaha
Sari tohmatay to hamaray hisay main ayi Hain
Ab insaaf mangay kaha Jain hum
Yahaan sub ne apnay asal chehray dikhain Hain
Yahaan insaaf milnay Ka koi wqt muqarar nhi hota
Insaaf ke intazar main logoo ne kitnay log dufnaii Hain
 is tanqeed ki gutan se bachnay ke liye
Humnay mout ke kya kya zaryay azmai Hain
Bs umeed Allah se ha ek din unka bhi hisaab Hoga
Jin nay humain ye simat dikhai hain.

# Toiba Bilal

- This is Toiba,17years old.
- She is in love with poetry.
- One day she was thinking about her future,she was very worried.
- On the other side she was very excited to write her own book of poems,but because of her study and other personal problems at first she ignored her passion.
- With the flow of time,she again started thinking about the world of poetry.
- And on 15-03-2020,she wrote her first poem"Erring regret".
- According to Toiba, "The best way to express our happiness, concern and all other feelings is only poetry.

# The Blockade sphere

Rubbing her burned heel
Just like banana peel
She can't express,frailish zeal
Covered her mouth with seal
What all going,no one can feel
Became her life a stopped wheel
a broken wheel.

# Rape : The Felony

The bloody stone
The slud shown
The male unknown
The fusk in cone
Her broken bone
Her wounded tone
Her garb blown
Her fame flown.
The huge atone
Never condone.

# Yogesh Gurjar (Chinu)

मेरा नाम योगेश व निकनेम चीनू है। 1200 से ज्यादा quotes & poetry लिख चुकी हूँ, 40 Anthology Book & E-Book में काम किया है Co-Author के रूप में। पहली बुक writer के रूप में "सच्ची बातें चीनू" है।

पहले किसी एक ने जिस्म को तार तार कर दिया,
फिर हजारों की नजरों ने जीना दुश्वार कर दिया,
ताने मारने वालो ने जीना मुहाल कर दिया,
गन्दी नियत वालो ने गन्दी नजरों से देखना शुरू कर दिया,
मै रोई तो दिलासा देने वालों की भीड़ इकट्ठा हो गई,
फिर सरेआम मेरी रूह का व्यापार कर दिया,
गलती निकाल दी मुझमें ही
गुनाहगार को बेगुनाह बता दिया,
तमाशा देखने वालों की भीड़ थीं,
मगर सब कुछ देखकर भी चुप रहने वालों की तादाद थी,
बोला ना किसी ने एक शब्द भी,
हैवानों को सब यूँ ही छोड़ देते हैं,
गुनाहों की तादाद इसीलिए बढ़ रही हैं,
खुद की बेटी बच जाये बस इसी सोच में रहते हो,
दूसरे की बेटी की इज्ज़त लूट जाये बस यही चाहते हो...!

 उड़ने आई थीं शहर में,
सपनों को पूरा करने आई थी शहर में,
पता नहीं था लोगों की नियत खराब है शहर में,
लड़की को अकेला देखकर मौका समझते हैं,
गिद्ध की तरह उस पर टूट पड़ते हैं,
बेआबरु करके उसे छोड़ देते हैं,
वो उड़ने आई थीं उसके पँखों को ही तोड़ देते हैं,
हराम कर देते हैं उसकी जिंदगी
बिलखती, तड़पती उसे छोड़ देते हैं,
जीते जी मर जाती हैं वो,
जीने की आस भी वो छोड़ देती हैं,
लोग ऐब निकाल देते हैं मुझमें ही,
मेरे कपड़ों पर ताने कस जाते हैं,
भूल जाते हैं उस 6 महीने की बच्ची को भी
जिस पर वात्सल्य की जगह वासना तुम्हारी फुट पड़ती हैं...!!

# Zaid Jardosh

Zaid is pursuing his bachelorette in Microbiology and is obsessed with inking poetries. His dedication and passion towards poetry made him a poet.

The Darkened clime
in peak of the night
cerebral spine
aching alone in
spheres of forlorn
those numbing feels
are unable to heal
suppressed screams
still echoes aloud
bursting thy lungs
threatening thy fear
crawl in collapsing sheer
eyes sick and dried in tears
soul seems confined
in thy darker shades
hues of life are slowly getting fade
fenced by that cunning demonic face
conferred with bulk of hate
the hell of fires
seems to be made for 'em
for they satisfy their lust
on skin of the sinless souls
to fulfil their desires as whole
the hope is still alive till morn
tearing thy darkness, dawn is on way
soul sits in between, thy agony
of past and doubted tomorrow
Will the sun rise?
Or the whole life will end
with these hidden bruises and scars.

# Zara Ayman Soofiyan

This is Ayman Gulzar ,19 years old. She loves to exaggerate everything in a brief manner,so she chose the world of poetry. She started writing these beautiful lines from 9-sep-2019. First of all she wrote some beautiful lines about herself.

# <u>Roothi Huwi Taqdeer</u>

Mai tooti howi ek jaan hu
Mai roothi howi ek jaan hu
Meri har saans dafan hai yu
Meri har wafa juki hai yu
Hai meri zindagi pyaas jesi ab
Ki darya bhi hai rootha mujh say
Ki sehra hai meray hamdam
Ki mai tooti huwi ek jaan hu
Mai roothi huwi ek jaan hu
Ki har koi hai shikwa karay mujh say
Meri tamannaoo k qaatil hai sab
Ki har lehar hai mujh say khafa
Ki mai tooti huwi ek jaan hu
Mai roothi huwi ek jaan hu
Ki naraz hai mera har pall
Ki choota huwa mera har kal
Meri ibtida bhi roothi si
Meri intiha bhi bhi tooti si
Ki mai tooti huwi ek jaan hu
Mai roothi huwi ek jaan hu.

## <u>Khoyii si ek beti</u>

Bikhra sa saaz hu mai
Dabi huwi awaz hu mai
Mai hu chup si, Kyun hu jhuk si
Hasi mai bhi hai meri khoof sa
Sadaye meri hai tadapti huwi
Meri har cheekh hai matam yu
Mera din bhi hai jesay raat
Koi haseen lamh na mera huwa
Hai kyu meri zindagi aisi
Ki muskurahat bhi meri udasi jaisi
Ek arsay say hu mai ye soochtii

Ki hu kya mai ek boojh jaisi
Ki hu sab k dil mai ek muflis jaisi
Ki saari qainat mujhse khafa jaisi
Mai maa hu,hu mai ek beti
Rahu har pal ye sochti rehti
Meri duniya hai alag jaisi
Ki koi yagana nahi mera
Ki bikhra howa saaz hu mai
Dabi huwi awaz hu mai

Flairs and Glairs, a platform by a student for the students. We are esteemed youth struggling to carve out our path for our future and we follow a basic mindset Since everyone is not born with all-round skills. Joining hands with people who are born to execute it with perfection is the best way to evolve. Self-Evolution is the need of the hour but, evolving as a community is what we strive for. The initiative as kickstarted by, Founder- Mr. Shubham Shah with the motive to utilize the skillset and talent of writing has now a team of 10+ people who are actively participating into newer forms of learning and discovering talents among youngsters. We Provide platform and services like Publishing opportunities, Open mics, Workshops, Hands-on training. Operating with Brand Name of Flairs and Glairs (Publication House), we offer the chance of elevating a passionate writer to an esteemed author With Brand name Teekhe Zasbaaat. We bring to you an opportunity to get accustomed with the Public Speaking and Presenting of Thoughts along with regular challenges to brush up your inking spirit. The newest initiative to extend our services we introduced in a new writing Platform- The Glittering Fables and Ink Over Tears.

*We Choose to Fly Like A Falcon than to be*

*a Leg Pulling Crab.*

To Know More:  Infoline – 7781900870
Mail Us At-
flairsandglairs@gmail.com / info@flairsandglairs.in
Or Visit is at
www.flairsandglairs.com / www.flairsandglairs.in
Social Handles- @flairsandglairs @teekhezasbaaat